Amelia the Flying Cat
Copyright © 2017 by Nikki Floreno.
All rights reserved. Printed in China.
Published in 2017 by Fables & Fauna

Library of Congress Control Number: 2017939389
ISBN 978-0-9988364-0-9

Summary: "Falling is never easy. Especially for Amelia, since everyone but her is a bird and can fly!
Amelia tries, but can a cat really fly without wings?"

Edited by Douglas Humphries & Emmy Scott. Design & Cover by Nikki Floreno. Text, 15 pt Short Stack.
The illustrations in this book were created with ink, markers, and colored pencils.
Thank you to our Kickstarter backers for helping Amelia fly!

First Edition.

Amelia

THE Flying Cat

by Nikki Floreno — Nikki Flo ♡

Fables & Fauna
Georgia

Amelia lived up in Bird Tree Town,
where all the birds lived in their
nest neighborhoods.

But Amelia wasn't like
the other birds.

She was a cat.

Cats don't have wings
like birds do.
That's why cats can't fly.

But Amelia wanted to
fly like a bird anyway!

Then she could be like her parents.

When she put on her mom's pilot goggles, Amelia felt like she really could fly!

Every day at flight school,
Amelia played with the birds her age.
They were all learning how to fly.

One by one,

Each of them flew,

For the very first time.

All of them,
except for Amelia.

Amelia wanted to fly like a bird,
but how could she fly without wings?

She decided to make her own wings!
Her parents were happy to help.

There are a lot of different types of wings,
so Amelia tried each one.

First, she tried
feathered wings,

But she fell
with a "splat!"

Next, she tried a
hang glider,

But she went
down with
a "ker-plop!"

She even tried
using balloons,

But they went
"pop, pop, pop!"

Finally, she tried
a propeller plane,

But she
dropped with
a "bam!"

Cats can't fly.

And neither could Amelia.

"We can be your
wings,"
her dad said.

"Hold on!"
her mom said.

For the first time,

Amelia saw the world.

There was so
much to see!

They flew by
trees of all
shapes and
sizes.

They flew by
tall snow
capped
mountains.

They flew by
tropical
beaches with
waterfalls.

Amelia wanted to explore each place,
but she was too high up and far away.

Amelia thought,
"Why fly by the world? I want to see
what's inside the world!"

Suddenly, Amelia wished she wasn't flying.

She wished she was exploring the world below.

That's when she knew
it was time to stop
flying like a bird,

And to start being
curious like a cat.

Her parents were so proud of her!

After falling again and again,
Amelia finally fell into what
she was meant to do.

Explore the world.